I0575506

Sunrise at The Nook and Cranny Café

A COZY MAGICAL ROMANCE

KELLY FAE WILSON

A TIDE OF PEOPLE flowed around Niamh. She stood alone in the rush on the sidewalk, face lifted to catch the colors of the rising Santa Monica sun. No one else stopped to witness the daily miracle of morning. Phones open, earbuds in, to-do lists circling like vultures over their heads, they plunged past her.

Niamh missed having someone to notice the sunrise with.

She sighed, moved off the sidewalk, and pulled open the door to her café. The kitchen of The Nook and Cranny clinked and sizzled, breakfast already in full swing. When Niamh and her late husband, Oisin, had first opened the café, they'd been the ones in at four am. Now she had a full staff and the luxury of arriving later. In her office, she exchanged her jacket for an apron and opened the curtains. The sunrise she'd left on the sidewalk flooded across her desk, highlighting a stack of documents.

Niamh threw a glance at the sky. "Yes, I know. I don't need a reminder, thank you." The documents spelled out an offer to buy her café, and time was almost up to make a decision. "Almost," she said. "But not quite. I still have until Friday."

Goosebumps rippled up her arms, and she shimmied into the chunky cardigan hung on the back of her office door. Her staff often teased her about her sweaters—*You're thirty-seven, not sixty-five. Wear something cute!*—but Niamh was always cold, and the sweaters felt like comfort blankets. Or armor.

She rolled up the offer papers, shoved them deep in her apron pocket to ruminate upon, and exited her office. Leaning against the hallway, she surveyed her culinary kingdom as the breakfast crowd filled the booths. From her vantage point she saw the whole room but remained out of sight herself.

The customers couldn't see much of each other either. Clever design had placed the freestanding, C-shaped booths in an array that limited the view of the other booths. This privacy was one reason The Nook and Cranny tended to attract celebrity clientele from the city's film industry—they could eat without someone else taking note of their every forkful.

The café's ambience figured into its five-star ratings as well. An indoor stream meandered through the space, ferns lining the raised sides and butterfly koi streaking like comets to the pond along the back. Floor to ceiling windows on the west wall highlighted the California coast, and off the main eatery, a library offered cushy armchairs and full bookshelves to savor with pastries and hot chocolate.

Privacy and ambience aside, Niamh liked to think that her signature herbal tea blends were also part of the reason people loved The Nook and Cranny. Her fingers found the documents in her apron. The tea and other recipes would go with her if she sold; those weren't part of the deal.

Which meant she could start over somewhere.

She loved this place, but the threads of the past tangled in her feet, tripping her when she tried to tread new ground. Her toes couldn't find any purchase. She knew the place loved her back too, but lately, if she left a jar on one shelf, it had moved to another when she came back for it. Her office chair, comfortably molded to her body when Oisin had still been alive, now poked her spine and cramped her hips.

Like nothing fit anymore. *Or I don't fit.*

The newest member of her waitstaff exited the kitchen, balancing a tray of French toast with violet and blueberry syrup.

"Trevor." Niamh halted him with a soft hand on his shoulder, recognizing the order. "Is that for Booth Four?"

He nodded and swallowed, looking nauseated. It was only his first week, and he'd no doubt heard the other staff talking. Booth Four, or Mortimer Abrams the retired film critic, was a regular. Over his years as a customer, he and Niamh had settled into a game. She always called him Booth Four, and he always mispronounced her name, calling her "Ni-am," instead of "Neev." But Tuesday mornings meant Booth Four was recovering from his Monday evening visits to the care center where his father suffered Alzheimer's. The stress tended to leak out over anyone who got near.

She took pity on Trevor. "I'll take it. You take booth seven. They won't bite."

"Thanks." He handed her the tray, shoulders sagging in relief.

"No problem." She carried the order to the floor.

"Morning." Niamh wrapped the word around Mortimer like a cozy blanket and slid the plate of French toast in front of him.

He grunted. Thick eyebrows pulled together, his mood spiking out like thorns in a bramble patch. She waited while he lingered over his first bite. The thorns mellowed to a smooth vine, and he finally answered, "Morning, Ni-am," before tucking into the rest of the stack. She patted his shoulder and moved on. Another regular waved to her from the front door, and she wove through the booths to greet him.

"Hey, Ian. How was the shoot yesterday?" She led him to his usual booth with a view of the bay.

"Productive," he said, laughing. "Which, considering how many people we had crammed on set, is saying something. I think we must be setting some kind of record for how many trailers are on the lot." He settled into the booth.

"Lovely. I suppose the producers, per usual, said no photos on set?" Niamh smiled conspiratorially. She hadn't seen the series that Ian was starring in, but she'd heard the buzz, and he loved to share with her. "And, per usual, you ignored them?"

Ian's eyebrows shot up in exaggerated innocence. "I have no idea what you're talking about." He slid his phone across the table.

Laughing, Niamh scrolled through photos of cast members pulling faces, and selfies with elaborate sci-fi set pieces. "Nice."

Ian took the phone back and pointed to one of the pictures. "He's actually joining me for breakfast today. Should be here any minute." He looked at her expectantly, and Niamh wracked her brain for the other actor's name, trying to look impressed.

"Oh, great. That's the guy from ... I think I saw him in ..."

"It's Rhys Morgan. *Cinema Today's* Charismatic Person of the Year?"

"Right, yes. Rhys Morgan."

Ian shook his head. "Don't worry about it, Niamh. It's part of the reason we all love you. Where would we be without this place to eat in peace?"

The contract rustled in her pocket. *You might get an answer to that question sooner than you think.* She gazed out the wide windows to the bay, watching the selkie-shaped foam topping the breakers. Where would she be without this place? Where *could* she be?

"You ok, Niamh?" Ian asked.

"Yes." She cleared her throat. "Yes, I'm fine. Did you want to order for your friend or wait until he gets here?"

Ian pursed his lips, thinking. "How about my usual for both of us? But Rhys just got dumped. Any helpful tea suggestions?"

She clucked sympathetically. "I'll put something to-gether."

"Thanks." He nodded, and she headed to the kitchen.

The main prep area bustled with employees—they'd all keep their jobs if she sold, the contract specified that—but she ducked into the smaller side kitchen reserved for her. Glass jars of dried herbs lined wooden shelves, and an east window washed the work counter in natural light. She pulled out a leatherbound book of recipes and research, her own personal tea grimoire, and consulted her notes.

Niamh hummed as she worked, threading intention through the herbs she selected off the shelf. Hawthorn for resiliency, lemon balm for peace, and dried citrus peel for a brightness of hope. She passed over her usual bone china teacups, brewing the mix in a moss green, hand thrown mug and ...

Her fingers stilled.

Oisin had made that mug. But he'd been gone seven years. Seven years and a day, if she was being exact—his father had called last night to commemorate with her. Keeping Oisin's things on a shelf helped no one. Besides, he would want it to bring someone else comfort.

Steam rose from the steeping tea and stroked her cheeks, ran fingers through her hair. She closed her eyes. Saw Oisin's face, saw his happiness about where he was now. Then she let the image go. Just like she had let him go. Niamh set the mug down. She ran her fingers over the whorls in the wooden counter, debating yet again if she could truly let The Nook and Cranny go as well.

"Still time, still time," she murmured, drizzling honey from the hive in the café's garden into the green mug. Weaving back through the main kitchen, she picked up the rest of the order for Ian and his friend and headed back to booth two.

The other actor had arrived while she'd been in her kitchen. Rhys, she reminded herself. Rhys Morgan. Some people liked to be acknowledged by name, even while enjoying the privacy afforded by the café, while others preferred the staff pretend that they hadn't already seen their face on a dozen billboards that morning on the way to work. She'd forgotten to ask Ian which Rhys would prefer.

Niamh was accustomed to celebrities looking a cut above normal. Hair and clothes out of magazines, faces straight out of, well, the movies. Rhys Morgan was no different—beautiful cheekbones, a trim fashionable beard, and action-star physique set off by a form fitting green tee shirt and brown leather bomber jacket—but halfway across the room she scuffed to a stop, her breath caught in her throat.

Life and energy shone from his face, like the noon day sun had just walked into her restaurant. The *pull* of him was palpable, and she dug her heels into the floor to keep from leaning forward. If this was Rhys Morgan dealing with heartbreak, she was afraid to see him happy. No wonder that magazine had called him charismatic.

Rhys sat across from Ian, throwing agitated gestures around while he spoke. It wasn't difficult to overhear their conversation as Niamh approached their booth.

"Why are they allowed to dictate who I go out with?"

Ian nodded. "You should ignore them."

"I mean, if a group of people did this to someone who wasn't famous, it'd be harassment. They could sue."

"I know, man. Look, I know you're ticked that she dumped you first, but—"

Rhys cut him off. "She didn't just dump me, Ian. It's not like I've never been dumped before. Tildale and the gossip mill bullied her into it. All those articles questioning our relationship, and idiots cyberbullying her saying she wasn't 'pretty enough' to date me? That she made me 'look bad'? What kind of bull is that? You know what she actually said? She said she felt 'dim' next to me. How messed up is that? That they made her think that about herself?"

As Niamh set the tray on their table, brightness flared out of Rhys, like a solar flare, woven through with that *pull*. She blinked against it. Next to that glare, she could understand his former girlfriend's sentiment.

"I imagine most women couldn't stand next to you without feeling dim, or worrying they were making you look bad." The words slipped out unbidden, and she sucked in a sharp gasp, surprised at herself.

"What?" Rhys turned clear, blue eyes on her.

"Sorry," she stammered. She set the plates and mugs in front of Ian and his friend to distract from her blunder. "Scrambled eggs with parmigiano and herbed focaccia."

"Rhys," Ian jumped in. "This is Niamh Banwell. She owns this place."

Rhys was still staring at her. "Why would you say that?"

Niamh flushed. *Good question.* Much of her clientele came for privacy. She knew things about her regulars, but only because they trusted her and volunteered the information. Ian liked to talk, and over the years they'd formed an easy friendship. But other than that, she did not interfere in customers' conversations. She didn't know what had possessed her to speak just now.

"Apologies, Mr. Morgan." She picked up the empty tray and changed the subject. "Ian asked for something special for you, said you had a bit of a broken heart. The tea may help with that." She nodded to Oisin's green mug, trying to redirect the focus to the food.

Rhys didn't take his gaze off her. "I'm not actually heartbroken. We weren't a good match, but that should be for her and me to decide, not the internet."

"Of course." Niamh started to back away, but Rhys wasn't finished.

"And why should 'most women' worry about making me look bad? Or any woman? Would *you* worry about making me look bad if we were on a date?"

Niamh glanced at Ian for help, but he leaned back in his seat, the corners of his mouth twitching upward as he watched Rhys' tirade.

"Well," she hedged. "I suppose I don't have to worry about it because I wouldn't be on a date with you."

Rhys spread his hands. "But why wouldn't you? This is exactly what I'm talking about. You already think I'm out of reach because the media makes it seem that way. But if I were just some guy who asked you out, you wouldn't be worried about 'making me look bad.' It'd just be a normal date, right?"

"Well, if this were some alternate universe—" she qualified her answer, not wanting it to appear as if she thought he *was* asking her out "—and we went on a date, I think you'd be the one making me look good." She gave a half laugh, to make it a joke.

Rhys shook his head. "Why should it have to be an alternate universe? Why couldn't I ask you out in this universe?" His voice rose, and a few heads poked around the edges of their booths.

Booth Four scowled at Rhys. "Niamh, is he bothering you?"

Rhys didn't notice the attention. "Why should the tabloids get to decide who I ask out?"

"I suppose you can ask out whoever you want," Niamh said slowly, waving off Booth Four.

"Great." Rhys took a long swig of tea and thunked the mug back on the table. "I'll pick you up here later this evening. About seven?"

"Oh. Oh! I ..." Her hands fluttered, and she clutched them together. "I don't ..."

Rhys rose from the booth. He stood at least six inches taller than her own five foot six. The heat of him crackled in the air, and Niamh backed up, afraid of being singed.

"There's a spot on the beach I like to walk, will that be ok?" he asked.

"The beach?" She threw one last desperate look at Ian, but he just shook his head, making no attempt to hide his laughter.

"Perfect. Niamh." Rhys nodded to her and pulled his jacket on. "I will see you this evening."

He downed one more swallow of tea, clapped Ian on the shoulder, and strode out the door, leaving his breakfast steaming on the table.

Baffled, Niamh watched him go. The light in the room dimmed as the door shut behind him. She picked up

Oisin's mug. Tiny sparks of light jumped from it to her hand, pricking her skin.

"Ian?" she asked. "What just happened?"

He wiped tears of laughter from his eyes. "Rhys. Rhys just happened."

The Nook and Cranny closed at 4 p.m. Niamh walked the two blocks to her apartment, showered and opened her closet. What did one wear for a walk on the beach with a movie star on the rebound? She decided on a pale-yellow dress with a floral print, and sandals. And a sweater.

She examined herself in the bedroom mirror and almost switched outfits, but the contract rattled in the pocket of her jacket from where she'd hung it over her desk chair.

"Right, you've more important things to think about," she scolded herself. *He probably won't even show up. Even if he does, it was a passing whim. Nothing more.*

She settled on the couch with her laptop and a fleece throw to sip ginger hibiscus tea out of Oisin's mug. The flecks of light still clinging to the cup had nothing to do with why she'd brought it home with her. Of course not. She had simply felt like it and that was reason enough.

Half an hour passed browsing through real estate sites in various cities, hoping to find a place that sparked something in her. When she was done, she took her time walking back to the café, not wanting Rhys to find her waiting and think her overeager.

She was early anyway.

A breeze blew up the street, and she shivered. Pulling her cardigan around her tighter, she sat on the low wall in front of her restaurant to let the late evening sun warm her back. A Western fence lizard scampered through the creeping fig that grew up the stone.

"Oh, hello." Niamh leaned toward it. "My apologies, sir. Did I push you out of your sunbeam?" The lizard performed a series of furious pushups.

A shower of sparks, like molten drops of sunlight, fell next to her, and a voice spoke over her shoulder. "What are you watching?"

Niamh jumped. Rhys stood next to her, peering into the leaves, a backpack slung over one shoulder. Niamh slid off the wall, mouth open. Did he know he radiated this light? This heat?

He laughed. "You look surprised to see me."

She shrugged and rubbed her arms where his sunlight clung to her sleeves. "I wasn't entirely sure you were serious."

"Very serious." Despite his words, his cheeks lifted like he was trying not to laugh. "Unless there's some legitimate reason you and I should not go out tonight? Mob ties? Bodies buried in the garden?" The fence lizard scurried out of hiding and down the wall. "Overprotective pet reptile?"

She shook her head, unable to hide a smile at his joking. "No, none of those."

"Excellent. In that case, our destination is just a short walk from here." He waved down the street toward the boardwalk, and Niamh fell into step beside him.

"It's kind of funny," Rhys said. "I come to this beach pretty often, but I'd never been into your place before. Ian found out and said I had to come check it out." The shops ended, and their footsteps echoed on the planks of the boardwalk. The sunset blushed and blazed over the ocean, unapologetic in its brilliance. Rhys stopped to watch. "I'm glad I finally got a chance to."

Niamh hesitated, unsure what he could be glad about already. She tried for a joke. "Yes, next time you'll have to actually try the food."

He tossed his head back, laughing. Shafts of light burst off him like confetti and settled in Niamh's hair.

"True," he said, still laughing. "The tea this morning was great, but I guess I was too fired up to eat."

"Don't worry about it," she said gently. "It's awful what they did. You shouldn't be harassed like that." At the end of the walkway, she slipped her shoes off. Warm sand cradled her feet, and her shoulders relaxed. A pair of seagulls hopped out of their path.

Rhys ducked his head. "I appreciate that. Anyway, you're being a good sport about my unconventional invitation this morning."

"Conventional is overrated. And Ian's been a good friend to me, I'm sure he'd give me a heads up if he thought you were too out there," she teased.

He laughed again. "I'm sure he would. Here we are." Rhys plunked down in front of a grouping of boulders, facing the ocean, and began pulling art supplies out of his backpack. Niamh sat next to him and trailed her fingers through the sand. The selkie shapes from this morning were back. They flipped their tails playfully at her before merging with the other waves and washing on shore.

"Here." Rhys handed her a flat wooden board, thick blank paper, and a box of pastels. "The sunsets here are the best. The game is to try to capture it on paper before it's over."

She looked at him, pleasantly surprised. "That sounds like a lovely game." One that noticed a moment, that noticed the sun. She wondered if Rhys liked sunrises as much as he liked sunsets. "You're an artist then?"

He pulled a face. "Not remotely. Most of my 'games' end up gracing the walls of my trash can."

"Why do you do it then? Play this game if you're not going to keep your art?" Niamh selected an apricot-colored stick and stole a sideways glance at him. His fingers were poised over his paper, but his eyes roved over the sea.

"Everything I do is on display." He looked at her, expression earnest. "Don't get me wrong—I love acting. *That's* my art, and I'm so lucky that I get to do it. I wouldn't change it for anything. But it's always there, for anyone and everyone to see. Casting directors, producers, directors, film critics, the audience. And everybody's got an opinion on what I do. That gets really ... loud."

Niamh nodded. "That sounds like quite a lot of pressure."

"But with this," he held up a pastel stick, "no one sees it. It can be as awful as I want and there are no consequences. I'm allowed to be bad at it. I can put googly eyes and a mustache on that sun because I don't have to show it to anyone if I don't want to, and no one gets to have an opinion about it unless I let them."

"I understand." Reviews of her café might be on a smaller scale than what Rhys dealt with, but they did impact her livelihood, and she knew what that pressure felt like. "Outlets are important. And the tabloids can't pressure your pastel sun to break up with your paper, can they?" she joked. Rhys laughed.

He did that a lot. Laugh. But it was warm and unapologetic, like the sunset.

They drew quietly for a while, side by side, not quite touching. The last rays of the sunset warmed Niamh's face, and Rhys' heat warmed her side. She slipped her cardigan off, surprised to find she wasn't cold.

"Ok, Niamh of The Nook and Cranny." Rhys played a drumroll on his knees. "Moment of truth." He held out a hand for her drawing.

She gave it over with a laugh. "No judgment, right? I'm not much of an artist either."

"None whatsoever. But look at that! You've got all kinds of artistic things going on here. There's balance and interesting texture and is that ..." He squinted at the paper. "Is that Elmo's face in the sun?"

"What?" She snatched the picture back, examined it and grimaced. "Ok. I grant that the darker smudges of red do sort of, *kind of*, resemble a face. But it's not Elmo."

Rhys fell into a laugh again, head leaning back on the boulder. Niamh wondered that the sand beneath him didn't melt and turn to glass under the heat radiating from that laugh.

She couldn't help but laugh with him. Whatever she'd expected from a date with an A-list movie star, it wasn't this easiness. "Alright then, let's see yours."

He handed over his paper, wiping tears of mirth from his eyes. He had followed through on his earlier threat and drawn a melodrama-villain mustache and a top hat on the sun.

"Ha!" She gave it back. "Destined for the Louvre, we are."

Rhys sat back up, a grin still crinkling his cheeks. "Oh, yes. I'm sure they'll give us whatever the art world's version of an Oscar is."

Niamh watched his face glow, feeling that pull burn along her skin. "You have a beautiful smile."

Rhys tilted his head, his smile softer, but didn't speak, and she flushed.

That's the second time I've blurted out a completely inappropriate comment around this man. She switched to a teasing tone to distract from what she'd said. "That means when you're older, your wrinkles will be in the right places."

Rhys just nodded. "I hope so."

"Excuse me?" A woman approached them, a boy who looked about eight years old hiding behind her. "Would you mind if he got a picture with you? You're his favorite character." She pushed her son forward a step. Niamh thought the boy looked like he might throw up.

"Oh my gosh, your tee shirt is so cool!" Rhys pointed at the boy's superhero shirt. "Is he your other favorite character?"

The child nodded and grinned. "I love how he squirts toxic slime."

"Man, me too." Rhys knelt next to the boy for the picture. "If I had to play a different guy in the same universe, it'd totally be him." Rhys pointed to the kid and looked at the camera with an amazed expression, like he was the fan meeting his hero. The mom took the picture and thanked Rhys. As they walked away the boy looked back, beaming.

Niamh wrapped her arms around her knees, watching him. "That was really kind."

Rhys shrugged. "Kids are the best fans. They know how to play way better than grownups."

The last of the color faded out of the sky, leaving the ocean dark. Small groups lit bonfires down the beach. Strings of electric lights lit up a square of food trucks at the top of the boardwalk.

Rhys packed up the art supplies and helped Niamh to her feet. "Are you hungry? I'm sure it's not as fabulous as what you serve, but the BBQ sandwich is pretty good." He nodded toward a truck with a grill logo.

"Sounds great."

When they reached the edge of the square, Rhys offered an arm to help her balance while she put her sandals back on. A harsh light flashed from the food truck closest to them, and Niamh blinked. A man with a long-lense camera gave a cheeky wave and sauntered off.

Rhys' arm tensed under her hand, and he glared at the man's back before turning to Niamh. "Sorry about that."

"Hardly your fault." She watched the photographer disappear beyond the circle of light. He would have snapped his picture when her hand was resting on Rhys' arm.

The line at the trucks was short, and they took their sandwiches to a low stone wall on a rise above the beach. Palm trees lined the walkway running behind the wall, fronds mimicking the low rushing song of the waves.

"What was her name?" Niamh asked between bites.

He didn't ask who she meant. "Tory."

"How did you meet?" Asking about exes wasn't the best idea on a first date, but this wasn't a *real* date. After all, Rhys had asked her, a complete stranger, out on impulse—as a reaction to his breakup. She reasoned he needed to talk about that more than he needed an actual date.

Rhys sighed, but even his sigh came out with a little chuckle. "She had a small part on a project I was filming. She's actually a tennis player, but decided she wanted to try acting. The gossip mill kept saying things like she was 'too athletic' or didn't have the 'right look,' whatever that's supposed to mean. Total garbage."

"Absolutely," Niamh agreed. "You told Ian you were going to break up with her, though?"

He nodded. "Not because of what people were saying. We just weren't a good fit."

"Why not?"

He looked sheepish. "It might sound silly."

"You asked me out completely on the fly, and we drew funny sunset pictures," she pointed out.

Rhys scattered another sunshine laugh. "I guess that's true. Ok. Tory didn't like dogs."

"Ah, I see." Niamh nodded and deposited the sandwich wrappings in a trash can next to the wall.

"Really? You don't think that's a stupid thing to break up with someone over?"

"Not at all. What kind of person doesn't like dogs? Definitely speaks to me of trouble down the road."

"Yes!" Rhys' face grew animated. "Exactly. How can you not like dogs? It makes me think they're gonna be really fussy about other things too. And not liking animals is just so ..."

"Out of touch with the world?" she finished. A chill wind blew off the waves, raising goosebumps on her arms. The words echoed her own feelings too closely. She slid off the wall, removed her sandals again, and strolled toward the waterline, walking away from the offending phrase. She had options. The contract was waiting for her at home. If she were out of touch with this "world," this place, she could find a different one.

Rhys followed her, his shoes off too. He smiled and gold swirled around him like fireflies. "Yes, just like that. So you have a dog?"

"Sadly, not right now." She surreptitiously caught a few of the gold flecks out of the air and the chill dissipated. "My late husband and I had a beautiful shaggy mix of uncertain origin, but she died in the same car accident he did."

Rhys stopped. "Oh, wow. I'm so sorry."

"It's alright, truly. I feel them around every now and then. They're happy where they're at, and I'm glad they have each other for company." She bit her lip. Why was she talking about this? Surely he wasn't interested.

"What was his name?" He repeated her earlier question back to her. "If it's ok to ask?"

"It's fine. Oisin. His name was Oisin."

"Ocean?" Rhys asked, pointing to the water.

She smiled and sat cross-legged on the sand, just out of reach of the foam rolling up to grab at her bare toes. "Close enough."

Rhys sat next to her, legs stretched out long. The waves reached his toes. "How did you meet?"

She cocked her head at him. "Are you familiar with any Irish legends?"

"Not really, no."

"Niamh and Oisin were a great love story. Niamh was a faery creature from Tír na nÓg—the land of eternal youth. She appeared to Oisin one day and asked him to come with her to Tír na nÓg. Oisin went, and they were married. He left his family, his people. Left his whole world behind to join her in hers. When some mutual friends introduced Oisin and I, he couldn't believe we had the same names as the story. Thought it was a sign. We almost named the café Tír na nÓg, but in the end marketing won out and we went with something easier to remember and pronounce."

Rhys dug a stone out of the sand, rubbed it between his fingers. "What happened after that in the legend?"

Niamh sucked in a breath. "He died. After three hundred or so years, Oisin decided he missed his family and wanted to visit Ireland. Niamh gave him a beautiful horse to journey back but warned him not to get off the horse. If his feet touched the earth, time would catch up with him and he'd crumble to dust. But while on his visit, he saw someone who needed help, and being himself, leaned down to help them. The saddle broke, and he landed on mortal soil."

"Wow." Rhys pulled his legs in and rested his arms on his knees. "What happened to Niamh?"

She shrugged. "The story ends there. We never hear what she did after, or how she dealt with it. I've always wondered if, after Oisin's death, Tír na nÓg ceased to feel like home. Did she still feel like she belonged there without him? Did she look for someplace new?" Niamh let her words trail off, not sure if she was speaking about the legend or herself.

Rhys shook his head. "I don't know what to say."

"It's alright. There isn't much *to* say." She pointed between them and chuckled. "Tragic backstory and complicated love life. We're quite the pair, aren't we?"

He held her eyes, face alight. "Let's be a pair again tomorrow."

She gaped at him. Was he asking her out again? This evening had been a one-off reaction to exterior pressure. He didn't owe her another date. "Tomorrow?"

"Yeah, are you busy? This was the best conversation I've had in a while." His golden smile came out to play.

Niamh's heart thumped. *Am I busy? Just planning out a new life and possibly selling my old one.* "Yes, no, I don't think so." She cleared her throat. "I mean, I'm not busy. We can do tomorrow."

"Awesome." Rhys grinned, his glow lighting up the beach, and Niamh smiled back.

No, I'm not too busy for that smile.

While The Nook and Cranny's main kitchen prepped orders for the lunch crowd, Niamh worked in her kitchen, sifting through jars of dried herbs and flowers for a new blend, and ignoring the real estate papers lurking on her workbench.

The phone rang, the offering agent's name showing on the screen. She let it go to voicemail and tucked the contract into a drawer below her workbench.

A breeze blew in her open window, and she grabbed her sweater. *It's full spring. I shouldn't still be cold.*

She sank into her chair and dropped her head in her hands. She was always cold. It was time to bite the bullet and sign the papers. Go somewhere that didn't necessitate sweaters in May. *But No one else is still wearing sweaters. The climate isn't the problem.*

Oisin's green mug glinted from the messenger bag she'd brought with her that morning. She retrieved it, turning it over in her hands.

Gold glinted off the mug. The shadowed corners of her bench lightened. And a voice spoke behind her. "Knock, knock."

She turned. "Rhys?"

He leaned against the doorframe, a hint of uncertain copper in the gold of his smile. "Your chef said you'd be in here."

"Yeah, hi. Come in." She smoothed her hair, aware of how much makeup she wasn't wearing. "Did I mess up the time?" It would be just like her to lose track of the hour working on a new tea formulation.

"No, no, you're good." Rhys gripped a newspaper in his hand. "I just came by to see if you'd changed your mind. About going out tonight."

"Why would I do that? You don't have your own overprotective lizard, do you?"

In answer, he crossed the room and spread a tabloid on her workbench. The picture of her holding Rhys' arm was front and center, along with an article's worth of speculation about who she was and what she wanted from Hollywood's most eligible bachelor.

It was inane drivel. Whoever wrote it had no factual information; they were merely selling copy by using Rhys' face. She felt him watching her as she read, the light that had poured from him so freely yesterday now dampened. Indignation rose in her. How dare they throw a shadow over such a light?

She tossed the paper in the trash. "Sorry, haven't changed my mind. I'm afraid you're stuck taking a common café owner on a second date."

The shadow lifted, and he grinned, lighting up the corners of the kitchen. "Good." He didn't say any more, but he didn't look away either. Gold flared along his skin. Heat radiated off him, tugging on her like gravity.

Niamh found she didn't need her sweater anymore.

She hung it on the back of her chair and fiddled with her herb jars to break the pull of him.

Rhys inspected a container of dried leaves. "Yesterday, you made me tea specifically for a broken heart."

"That's right." Niamh pulled down a jar of mint and sniffed it. Put it back.

"So you make tea that helps people with whatever their problem is?" He leaned against the workbench, gaze focused on her.

She paused her search to watch his face. She never knew exactly how people would react to this part of her. Oisin had called it a gift. When asked about it, Niamh had always simply said that she saw what she saw—Rhys' light, the thorns from Booth Four, selkies in the ocean, all of it. It had always been there. It was how the world was for her. And she figured if she could use it to help someone, she should. "That's what I try to do."

"Fascinating. What are you working on? Can I help?"

"Really? Are you not filming today?"

He shook his head. "I have to shoot tomorrow, but today I'm off. I wouldn't mind hanging out here with you for a bit if I'm not in the way."

She swallowed. *It's ok. It's fine. It's just an impromptu date in between the first and second date. Date one and a half ...* "Sure. I'm working on a new blend. You can help me pick what to put in it if you like."

"Sweet." He rubbed his hands together. "Willing guinea pig at your service."

"I'm trying to make something that aids in decision making." She shot a glance at the drawer with the contract. "So far I've got cinnamon, for illumination, and snapdragon flowers preserved in honey, for reflection, but it's still missing something."

Rhys started the kettle heating on the stove, then came back to her side, shoulder touching hers as he leaned over to inspect jars. He lifted a few lids, sniffed experimentally. "How do you know which to choose?"

She shrugged. "There are plenty of books and things on herb lore, and I've studied those. But I don't necessarily follow them. I suppose I let, I don't know what you'd call it—maybe whim?—guide me when I'm blending."

He gave her an appraising look. "Maybe whim. Maybe intuition would be a better word, though." That pull tugged on her again. She dug her toes into her shoes to keep from sliding forward.

"Yeah, let's go with intuition." He broke eye contact and went back to investigating jars and crockery.

Niamh glanced away only to find the contract sitting back on her workbench. At the same moment she tried to gather the stack of legalese, Rhys reached for a jar of dried ginger. Their arms crossed, their elbows bumped, and the real estate papers fluttered to the floor.

Jump out and shout hello, why don't you? Pushy papers. If I put you in the drawer it's because I intend for you to stay in the drawer. Niamh bent to retrieve them, but Rhys beat her to it. He shuffled the papers into order, and Niamh saw the moment he understood what he held.

"Are you selling?" he asked.

"Maybe. I haven't entirely decided. I have to soon, though. That offer expires the end of business week."

"Yeah, that's not much time." Rhys gave a slight frown, but handed her the contract and returned to searching through herb containers. "So, I looked up that legend last night. The Niamh-Oisin legend."

She stashed the naughty papers in her desk, happy for the change in subject. "Did you? What did you find?"

"Well—oh, what about this one?" He proffered a jar for her to smell.

"Hmm, maybe." She shook a bit into a teapot along with the other herbs.

"Some of the commentary I read suggested that Oisin's death represented the demise of paganism, the old religion being supplanted by a new one."

Niamh poured boiling water into the pot and set it to steep. "Yes, I've heard that as well. I think it's sad." The new religion would not have approved of her gifts, nor of the things she saw in the world.

"I found another one that painted Niamh as some kind of temptress. Like she went to Ireland just to steal Oisin away from his family and his home."

"And what do you think of that idea?" She was herself, not the Niamh of legend, but that view of the story always put her back up.

"I think it's garbage." His eyes flicked to the tabloid in the trash can. "As if Oisin couldn't have actually fallen in love or made his own decisions. Niamh didn't steal anything. Oisin gave it freely and was happier with her. He found something he didn't know he was missing." Heat built on him, warming the small kitchen. He blew out a breath. "But like you said, I didn't find any versions that said what happened to Niamh. Which is kind of messed up. What, after Oisin died she didn't count anymore? Or wasn't capable of having a life of her own?"

Niamh strained the tea, drizzled in honey. "Perhaps the first interpretation was right—Niamh was part of the old, and the new thought she didn't belong. Perhaps the new couldn't even really see her properly, couldn't perceive her, to finish telling her story."

"Then that is a 'new' that isn't worth having." Rhys stepped close. "And maybe Niamh should decide on a different 'new.'" He handed her the mug of tea. "How is it?"

She sipped it, deliberately not looking at the drawer where she'd put the real estate papers. The tea went down discordant, the flavors not quite landing. "I think it still needs some work."

He nodded, took the mug back, and set it on the counter. He hesitated a moment, watching her face, then reached up to stroke her cheek once. "We can keep working on it. See you tonight?"

Warmth spread across her skin. "Yes."

"Niamh," Rhys stopped in the doorway and turned back, smile playful. "It'd be a shame if you sold this place. I just found it." He grinned and left, whistling.

She brought a hand to her face. Her fingers came away dusted with gold.

When Rhys pulled into the parking lot of a fun center, Niamh had to laugh. It was so ... Rhys. In the lobby, she took in the neon patterned carpet, 80s pop music echoing off the bowling lanes, and the smell of cheap nacho cheese.

"Wow, I haven't been to one of these in ages."

"Really?" Rhys led them to a hallway purple with black-lights. "Let's start with the best then. Go-karts are this way."

"Do you know, I've never actually done Go-Karts."

He stopped short. "Never?"

She shook her head.

"Never *ever*?" He gaped at her. "What kind of child-hood did you have?" He took her hand in his and struck a tragic face. "This is a travesty of Shakespearean proportions and we must remedy it. You're driving."

Niamh loosened her fingers assuming Rhys would let go once they started walking again. But he interlaced his fingers in hers, keeping her hand even after they arrived at the Go-Karts. His hand was warm, small calluses along the top of his palm rubbing comfortingly on her skin. She hadn't held hands with a man since Oisin. But she felt no recoil, no oddness, and she filed that away to examine later.

The line at the track moved quickly, but Rhys bounced in anticipation, like a kid with a pile of presents he had to wait to unwrap. Even under the blacklights, gold arced off him, shooting up to the ceiling. His eagerness was infectious.

"Which car?" she asked when the gate finally opened to allow their group on the track.

Rhys pointed to a red car. "That one, my favorite color."

"Alright, red it is." Niamh folded herself behind the steering wheel. Rhys had to bunch up his knees to fit and his hip pressed against hers. "Is there such a thing as being too old for these?" The rest of their group had to be twenty years younger.

He waved away the idea. "Nah. Being a grownup is overrated anyway. I try to avoid it whenever I can."

She laughed—a head-thrown-back-laugh—and realized it was the way Rhys laughed. When was the last time she'd laughed like that?

A buzzer sounded and the other cars zoomed past them. She yelped and Rhys, also laughing, gestured frantically at her feet. "The pedal, the pedal!"

She hit the accelerator. They shot forward. Rhys threw his hands in the air, whooping. It was no interstate, but the scale of the cars and the track made it feel like speeding, and Niamh whooped along with him.

The track curved, and she cranked the wheel to the left, sliding across the tiny seat, even closer to Rhys. He wrapped an arm around her shoulders and left it there on the straightaway. Niamh forced herself to concentrate on not hitting the other cars.

They made it around the track three times before the buzzer ended their turn. As Niamh pulled into the line of cars waiting to be returned, Rhys' arm tightened around her, the glee dropping out of his eyes.

She followed his gaze. "Is that ... the same photographer from the beach last night?" She squinted through the dim light.

Rhys grimaced. "Photographer is a generous word." He glared at the man for a moment but then his face cleared, and he hopped out of the car to hold out a hand for her. "Come on, laser tag is next."

In the laser tag briefing room, a teenaged attendant scrolled on his phone behind the desk. His face lit up when he saw Rhys.

"Hey, man, good to see you again."

"Robbie." Rhys smiled back and nodded to Robbie's phone. "Any progress since last time?"

The boy grinned. "She texted back a couple times."

"Sweet." Rhys gave him a fist bump. "How's it looking inside?"

"Good numbers for you tonight," the kid said. "Just four person teams."

"Perfect. Thanks, Robbie." He turned to Niamh. "Weeknights are less crowded, but I always let Robbie know when I'm coming, and he sets aside small teams that won't freak when they see this." He pointed at his face.

Robbie's lips twitched. "Yeah, your face is pretty freak-ish."

Rhys laughed and scratched his head. "It totally is. I can't figure out how I get the jobs I do."

Niamh laughed. "I like your face." She froze. Had she really just said that? *Out loud?* But Rhys' expression softened, and he leaned down to brush his lips against her forehead. Easy, natural. Like he thought this was their 20th date, not their second. Like how it felt to hold his hand.

She buckled on her laser tag vest, heart beating and fingers trembling. Robbie introduced the two other people on their team, but Niamh didn't catch their names. They held a brief strategy council and rushed into the course, her thoughts still swirling around the kiss on her forehead.

The room was set up like a maze, with a tower at each end. Three turns in, Rhys motioned for them to split up to cover both sides of a wall. He squeezed her hand and smiled before disappearing around the corner. Niamh followed suit, creeping around corners and feeling more than a bit silly. Laser tag was a first too.

Someone bumped her shoulder, and she stumbled back raising her gun. The person didn't step away.

"First time?" One of the strobe lights flickered over his face. The photographer.

Niamh swallowed. What was he doing in here? She lowered her gun and turned to go find Rhys.

The paparazzo followed. "It's just you look a bit awkward holding the gun."

Niamh ignored him and turned another corner, but nothing looked familiar.

"I'd say first time dating a celebrity too. Also awkward," he sang the last words like a joke.

She hit a dead end. The paparazzo was right behind her when she turned around. "Move." She tried to make it sound like a command, but her voice trembled, and her knees went rubbery.

He shrugged and stepped aside. "It'll always be awkward, you know. Trying to fit in with his world. All those parties and premieres, all the fancy people."

Niamh hurried past him.

A flash went off behind her. "All those cameras in your face."

She walked faster, struggling to hold down the bubble of panic in her chest. *Where's Rhys?*

"People questioning your motives. What *do* you want from Rhys Morgan, Ms. Banwell?" He was one step behind her, shooting taunts like they were still playing laser tag.

The panic bubble burst and she ran. Down a corridor, past a tower base, around a corner. She slammed into someone's chest and yelped.

"Whoa, whoa, what's wrong?"

Niamh sucked in a breath. Rhys. It was Rhys. His face turned to stone as he looked behind her, and she didn't have to answer his question. The gold streaks dancing off him sharpened to knife blades.

"Morgan," the photographer said. "Fancy meeting you here. Got time for a few questions?"

"Teeth, Tildale. Teeth." Rhys fixed him with a white-hot glare, and Tildale stepped back. Rhys took Niamh's hand and led her back to the briefing room. He spoke a few words to Robbie before they headed to the parking lot. On their way out, Niamh spotted a couple of beefy security guards on their way to the laser tag room.

"Niamh," he said when they'd reached his car. "I'm really sorry. Are you ok?"

He hadn't let go of her hand since leaving the laser tag course and the warmth of his fingers chased away the trembling in her stomach. "I'm fine."

"Are you sure? That wasn't exactly the ending I had in mind for the evening, but I can take you home if you want. Dealing with guys like that can be brutal."

"Who is he?" she asked.

"Alan Tildale. He writes—if you want to call it that—for that tabloid, StarWatch." His jaw tightened, and he glared back at the fun center as if he could hurl lightning bolts at Alan Tildale. The fire in his gaze made Niamh wonder if he could.

"What did you mean when you said 'teeth' to him?"

Her question pulled his gaze back and he chuckled, face lightening a bit. "Oh. The last time I talked to him I told him he has a few too many teeth in his mouth and I'd be happy to knock a few out."

Niamh couldn't help laughing. The image of Rhys punching Alan was all too satisfying. Rhys dropped her hand to open her car door, and cool night air flooded her skin like someone had thrown a bucket of water at her. She shivered.

Why didn't I bring a jacket? I always bring a jacket.

"Are you cold?" Rhys moved closer and rubbed her arms. Again it was natural, the slight hesitation he'd shown that afternoon before touching her cheek evaporated. His gravity pulled on her, his heat chased away the chill, and she realized why she hadn't thought to bring a jacket.

She found her voice. "I'm not cold when you do that. What was the ending you had planned for tonight?"

His eyes danced. "Ice cream from the concessions stand, of course."

She laughed. "Of course. Well, I don't think I want to go home just yet. I think if I tried to sleep now I'd just see that man's face. It's not fun center concessions, but I have scones at the café. And tea of course. If you want to do that?"

He smiled. "Sounds perfect."

As they drove out of the parking lot, Niamh glanced back at the fun center. The two security guards she'd seen were escorting Alan Tildale out the front door. She flipped around in her seat, but her neck prickled like Tildale was watching her until they drove out of sight of the parking lot.

Niamh unlocked The Nook and Cranny's front door and swept her hand along the wall for the light switch. She almost didn't need the lights; sun sparks danced off of Rhys, illuminating the entrance.

"Wow, I didn't see these before." He went to the stream and leaned over the edge to admire the koi. "They're beautiful."

Niamh joined him. "Our original idea was to do the salmon of knowledge, but koi proved more practical."

"Salmon of knowledge?" He looked at her, expression all little-boy curiosity.

"Yes. It's another Celtic legend. It was said that a salmon ate nine hazelnuts from nine trees and gained all the world's wisdom. The first person to eat the salmon would gain the knowledge for themselves."

Rhys chuckled. "Meaning that if one wants to be wise, one should eat at The Nook and Cranny."

She smirked. "Something like that." The koi gathered beneath them, lipping the surface of the water.

He dangled his fingertips in the water, letting the fish nibble at them. "Looks like the salmon are still hungry. I guess nine hazelnuts aren't that filling."

"That's the real secret," she laughed. "Koi are always hungry." She tossed them some pellets. "Shall we get some tea?"

He rose from his perch beside the stream and followed her to the kitchen. The real estate offer on the counter shifted and whispered. *Two more days. Two more days.*

Niamh laid a hand on them. *Shh. Be patient.* She sorted through jars, looking for a tea appropriate to the evening.

"Are you looking for this one?" Rhys picked up a mason jar that sat atop the contract.

She took the jar that had definitely not been there a second ago. "That's the one we were working on this afternoon. Still not finished. I was thinking of this one for now. Honeysuckle, jasmine and lavender." She put a kettle to boil.

"That sounds delicious." He tapped the papers, face thoughtful. "What will you do if you sell?"

Niamh stared at the decision blend. If she could finish it, she might have an answer to that question. "I was thinking of moving. Maybe. Find someplace where I can fit, where I belong."

"Moving, wow." He shook his head. "You know what's funny? I knew Ian had been coming here for a while, but I found two more people on set that come in for your tea. One for the Sunrise blend and one for the Wonder blend."

Niamh nodded. *Sunrise: citrus and mint to cheer and brighten. Wonder: jasmine and primrose blossoms to attract faeries.*

"They rave about the tea, about the food, about this place," Rhys went on. "And they say the owner is what makes it what it is. What is it that makes you feel like you don't belong here now?"

Niamh plated scones before answering, searching for the right words. "I was born in this city, raised here. I was married here, widowed here. I still have family near here. But so often lately I feel ... out of step. Like my clock is five minutes off from everyone else's. Or like one hand is taking lunch orders while the other is still mixing batter for breakfast?" She shook her head. "That sounds dumb. I don't know how to say it, but I'm still watching the sunrise while everyone else is already getting on with their day, and I just feel like I'm out of sync, or knocked out of orbit."

She bit her lip, wondering why she was sharing so much with a man who was practically a stranger. But then she remembered his lips on her forehead, his hand in hers. A stranger wouldn't feel so comfortable.

Rhys took the kettle from the stove and poured water into two mugs. "There's nothing wrong with watching the sunrise. Most people are in too much of a hurry anyway." He scooped up the plates of scones and continued, his tone lighter, "And I love breakfast for lunch."

She laughed, set the mugs on a tray and led him to the booth overlooking the bay. She'd turned on just the center lights when they'd arrived, but she didn't turn on the lights over the booth, preferring Rhys' brightness.

They ate in silence for a minute, watching the moon's reflection jump and dance on the ocean like some otherworldly hound. When Rhys scooted closer and slid an arm around her shoulder, the gravity of him pulled on her like the sun on the planets.

"What about here?" he whispered. "It feels like you could fit here."

Yes, she silently agreed. *It does.* Alan Tildale's taunts came back to her. *But could I fit in your world?*

"Why did you ask me out yesterday, Rhys?" She lifted her head, pulling back to look him in the eye. "I mean yesterday evening. The first time, at breakfast, I get that you were upset and wanted to prove a point. But after that, on the beach. Why did you ask me out again?"

He tilted his head. "Because I enjoyed our first date. Because I find you intriguing, and I want to know more about you. Isn't that usually why people go on a second date?"

It was such a normal answer. "Yes, I suppose that is why people go on a second date. And here, now?" She indicated his arm around her. "Is this usual for a second date too?"

He shook his head, face serious for once. "No. Not for me." He traced a finger along her cheek, and her heart sped up.

"So, what do we do about it?" she asked.

Rhys grinned. "We could go on a third date."

She laughed and leaned back into his shoulder. "That's a brilliant idea."

"Good. I have to work all day tomorrow till late, but we can do Friday?"

Niamh sucked in a breath. Friday. Decision day. But not seeing Rhys on Friday wouldn't help her decide about The Nook and Cranny. And she'd have all of Thursday to sort out her thoughts about selling.

"Friday it is."

Niamh blew out a breath and sagged against the wall in the short hallway. The clank of knives and forks jarred her bones. Conversation in The Nook and Cranny usually kept itself to a comfortable murmur, but today the volume had ratcheted higher and higher throughout lunch and the line of people waiting for a seat stretched out the door.

She knew why. Alan Tildale had released another article, with Niamh's name, the café's name, and a picture of her in the laser tag course looking like a deer in the headlights. None of the patrons waiting for tables were regulars. Instead, every time she crossed the room—which was often today as three of her wait staff had called in with the flu—heads swiveled, and the chatter picked up. The day had both dragged and trampled by, and she still hadn't had a moment to devote to the persnickety papers tucked in her apron pocket.

Trevor found her in the hall. "Booth five ordered but he wants to add something. I've got six, seven, eight, and nine already."

"Ok. I'll get it, Trevor." Niamh rolled her shoulders back and found her smile as she made her way across the room. The koi flicked their tails in protest of the chaos, splashing her arm, and she tossed in a few pellets to placate them before arriving at booth five.

Alan Tildale lounged in the booth, smirking. "Hey, there. I've heard you have *unique* teas. Could I get something for, say, uncovering someone's motives?"

Niamh's stomach clenched, but she lifted her chin. This was her restaurant. Her space. For now, at least. "What are you doing here?"

"Getting lunch. What are you doing here?" He gestured at her apron. "Aren't you supposed to be the owner? What are you doing waiting tables?"

Niamh didn't answer.

"This story just keeps getting better and better. It's like you're *trying* to give me headlines." He chuckled and spread a copy of the article on the table. "Rhys Morgan's new girlfriend, waiting tables. Is that why you're selling? Is the café in trouble?"

"I'm not his girlfriend." The answer came automatically. They'd been on a total of two dates. *And two … outside of date activities?* They had a third planned. But that was it. No relationship decisions made. Niamh's eyes flicked towards her lab kitchen, where the decision blend waited for her to work on it.

"Really?" Alan asked. "Fascinating. Why not? Is this just a fling for you? Your fifteen minutes? Do you think being seen with someone of his standing will get you a better price for this place?"

"What? No." Niamh flushed and took a step back.

"Why *are* you selling, Ms. Banwell? Public record has the former co-owner listed as your husband. Can't hack the world of sole ownership? I guarantee if you can't even handle the pressure of running a business, you'll never survive Rhys' world." He leaned forward, eyes narrowing. "Have you considered you could tank his career? You'll ruin his image, his reputation. You look ridiculous with him, you know. You'll never belong with him, with those people."

Her stomach turned watery. How had this man zeroed in so fast on her insecurities about belonging anywhere, let alone in company with someone like Rhys Morgan? She lifted her chin—he didn't need to know how close to the mark he'd hit. "You need to leave. Now."

He leaned back in the booth, an easy smile on his lips. "Oh, no, I'm still waiting for my lunch."

"But how will you eat it with no teeth, Tildale?" Ian's voice came from behind Niamh, and she turned in relief.

He nodded to her and faced Alan. "I'm eating here today, Tildale. I plan on being here for hours. You remember what a restraining order is, right? If I'm here, *you* can't be. And I'm afraid I can't vouch for the safety of your dentition if you stay." Ian bared his own teeth in a smile.

Alan glared at him but gathered his things and left. Niamh collapsed into the booth and dropped her head onto the table.

"Thanks, Ian."

"Anytime." He slid into the bench next to her. "Rhys asked me to check in."

Niamh lifted her head. "He did?"

Ian nodded. "He thought Tildale might pull something like this. He was the one that started all the online bullying when Rhys was dating Tory. The guy is seriously messed up. It's like he can't stand to see anybody else happy."

"Oh, wow." She glanced at the door Alan had stormed out of. "No wonder Rhys was so mad last night. He came by here yesterday afternoon, thinking I wouldn't want to go out again because Tildale had written that stupid article about our first date."

Ian sighed. "You should know Tory wasn't the first of his girlfriends to break up with him because of media pressure. You really don't follow celebrity news, do you?"

She shook her head, unsure if that was a point in her favor or if it meant she had no idea what she was getting into. "Do you really have a restraining order against Alan Tildale?"

"Yup. He kept following my kids to school, trying to get close to them."

Niamh's eyes widened in outrage. "Rhys is right. Alan has a few too many teeth in his face."

"Amen."

"Did Rhys," Niamh began. "Did he say anything else about me, when he asked you to check in?"

His eyes crinkled as he laughed. "Several things, which shall remain locked behind the gate of best friend confidentiality."

"Ian, come on."

He mimed zipping his lips, and she rolled her eyes. "Alright, fine. I imagine what you want for lunch is not nearly so secret?"

Still chuckling, he gave her his order. Niamh relayed it to the kitchen, told Trevor she was taking a break, and retreated to the safety of her lab kitchen.

She smoothed the offer papers out on her workbench. Creases cut deep across the pages, like a letter read too many times. It was a good offer. Fair to her employees, she'd keep her recipes, and the money was good. She wanted—needed—something new. A fresh sunrise, a new direction. A place to belong. With the payout she could start over someplace new.

So why am I stalling? Why can't I just sign this deal and get on with it?

There were people here she cared about, and people who loved The Nook and Cranny. But she couldn't visualize being here for the rest of her life. Had the Niamh of legend felt like she still belonged in Tir na nÓg after her Oisin died? It had been her home before she married Oisin, after all. She was a faery creature, from a faery world. Surely she hadn't rushed out into the human world searching for something new or different.

"Or maybe she did," Niamh muttered. "We don't have that part of the tale." If she had fled back to her mortal husband's world, would the Christian contemporaries have made her feel irrelevant and out of step, even while they recorded her story?

Alan Tildale's article from yesterday poked out of the trash can. Niamh narrowed her eyes at it. The monks hadn't really recorded Niamh's story. They told their own cautionary tale about a poor human man beguiled by a pagan creature and how it eventually ruined him.

She snorted. As if three dates could ruin an A-list actor's career. It was people like Alan Tildale that ruined careers.

Still, a shaky little voice in the back of her head told her part of what Alan had said was true. Chunky sweaters and tea mugs were not red-carpet material. She was an attractive woman, no ego and no false modesty. But she had no desire to wear the Botoxed, swollen-lipped look so prevalent in Hollywood, which meant she didn't look like she belonged in Rhys' world. And that world had chewed up and spit out far more confident people than her.

She blew out a breath and turned her attention to the decision-making tea blend. "What are you missing?"

Out the window, the midday sun glinted off basil leaves and warmed sage, calling her out to the garden. Niamh left the contract on the bench but brought the tea jar with her.

At the edge of the garden, she slipped off her shoes and socks. Holding the jar of dried herbs close to her chest with one hand, she stepped reverently between her plants, her free hand trailing over honeysuckle, hibiscus, and plum. The drone of bees in the orange blossoms quieted her worries. She crushed rosemary between her fingertips, breathing in its sharp scent. She closed her eyes, face to the sun, letting its heat smooth her forehead, and directed her thoughts to her tea, to the energy it should hold and what it should help people accomplish. *What do you need?*

Her phone buzzed.

Frowning, Niamh checked the screen. Her frown flipped to a smile. It was Rhys.

Hi, how you doing?

She snapped a picture of the garden and sent it. *Good. Just working outside.*

Wow! It's gorgeous. Maybe you can show it to me sometime?

Niamh breathed in the sunlight, imagining Rhys' sun sparks dancing through this space. *I'd like that. How's filming going?*

Pretty good. I even had a few minutes to practice my favorite allowed-to-suck-at-it hobby. Three laughing faces and a sketch of the director with a villain mustache followed, and Niamh burst out laughing.

Fabulous. Maybe don't let the director see it though.

She tapped a finger on the side of the phone, debating whether to bring up the confrontation with Alan—she didn't want Rhys to worry—but Ian would likely tell him anyway.

Ian came by. Thanks for sending him.

You're welcome. Did Tildale try anything? Frowny face.

He came in. Tried to pull more of the same. But Ian and I were able to make him leave, so it's all ok.

Three dots blinked on the screen while he typed. They disappeared. Reappeared. The text finally came through.

I'm so sorry, Niamh.

Don't be. It's not your fault Alan Tildale is a jerk. She changed the subject. *Excited to see what you've got planned for us tomorrow.*

Rhys sent a grinning emoji. *Go to bed early if you can. I have something really fun planned, but we have to go early. Pick you about 5 am?*

5 am? Now I'm really intrigued ha ha. Sounds good, I'll be ready. Meet at the café?

Café it is. Thumbs up. One more line came through. *I can't wait to see you again.*

She hugged the jar to her chest, reveling in the text with her face lifted to the sun. Something flashed to the left, and she snapped her head up. The fence between the garden and the side street shook, like someone had jumped off it. Footsteps pounded down the street. Niamh ran to check over the fence. The corner of a jacket disappeared around the corner. She thought she could guess who it belonged to, and her stomach sank.

She didn't know how Alan Tildale could twist a simple picture of her in a garden, but she had no doubt he would.

The moon danced between early morning stars in the west. On the way to The Nook and Cranny to meet Rhys, Niamh played at finding new constellations between the stars. Salmon, horse, tea mug. When she found a group of stars shaped like a mustache she laughed at herself.

At the café, a folded newspaper lay on the welcome mat. Niamh scooped it up, curious. The newspaper didn't usually get delivered this early. Her heart clenched when she unfolded it and saw StarWatch at the top.

The front page featured a full color photo of her in the garden, clutching the mason jar, face upturned and eyes closed with the headline, RHYS MORGAN'S GOLD-DIGGING GIRLFRIEND—LEADER OF A PAGAN CULT?

"Maybe you can wear a pointy black hat to your first premiere? Although I don't think the valets park brooms ..." Alan Tildale stepped out of the shadows, rubbing his chin thoughtfully.

Niamh's stomach turned watery. Her knees went wobbly. "What are you doing here?"

"I thought you'd like the first look at the article. You really do make it too easy." He grinned.

"You need to leave," she said, but her voice came out pinched. She scanned the article, keeping Tildale in her peripheral vision and the café door at her back. While never outright accusing her of brainwashing Rhys, the article heavily insinuated that she was taking advantage of him, and that if Rhys were in his right mind he never would have gone out with her.

The article was so obviously contrived that her knees regained some of their strength and her voice firmed. "Why do you even care? What does it matter to you what people do with their lives or who they date? What is the point of this?" She shook the paper.

"The point?" Alan sneered, stepping closer. "All these spoiled A-list phonies, strutting around like they're so far above the rest of us. There are no rules for them! DUIs, drug abuse, harassment, they get away with everything. *I* get slapped with restraining orders, but we couldn't possibly make *them* suffer any consequences, oh no!" He gestured wildly, face twisted. "The *point* is knocking them—and upstart, attention-seeking, gold diggers like *you*—" He jabbed a finger into her shoulder.

Niamh shoved it away. "Don't touch me."

"—back down to the dirt with the rest of us where you belong."

Tremors spasmed through her legs again. This close, she could smell alcohol on Tildale's breath.

Headlights pulled up at the curb.

"You. Need. To. Leave," she repeated, pointing down the street.

"No." Alan grabbed her wrist and twisted. Niamh slammed the heel of her other hand up into his nose, and he stumbled back, letting go of her wrist.

"Niamh!" A car door slammed, and Rhys was there next to her, looking her over, one warm hand on her cheek. "Are you ok?"

Alan growled, red dripping from his nose, and ran at them, fist raised. Rhys landed a solid punch to the side of his jaw, and the reporter fell to the ground. Something white and bloodied landed next to him. He shrieked and clambered to his feet, snatching his tooth from the ground.

"I'll sue! This is assault!"

"You attacked Niamh first, you moron. But you know what? Go ahead. We'll see what the judge says about you stealing pictures of people on private property." Rhys pointed to the photo of Niamh in her garden. "And we both know she's not the only one. I have so many people willing to testify against you, you'll never write another word the rest of your life. Get lost."

Alan waved his tooth in Rhys' face. "I'm not going anywhere! I'm calling the cops. And when they arrest you, I'll get the exclusive photos!"

Niamh backed against the café entrance, breaths shallow and quick. *How is this happening?*

The door pressed solidly against her back. A sudden breeze brought the scent of night blooming jasmine from the garden. On the stone wall, the fence lizard peeked its head out, disturbed by the commotion. An impression stole over her, as if the whole of The Nook and Cranny had wrapped its arms around her. *We've got you. Whether you stay or go, we've got you.*

Strength replaced the wobbly feeling in her stomach. She narrowed her eyes, straightening. How dare he? How dare this man come into her world and threaten her?

"No, you will not." She focused her will, just as she did when she poured intention into a tea. She drew it like a dagger, sharp and resolute, and aimed it at the pathetic man on the sidewalk. "This is *my* space." She stalked toward Tildale, pinning him in place with her glare, until her face was only inches from his. "Leave. Now."

Alan quailed. Turned. And ran.

"Oh my goodness ..." She let out a breath and let herself fall onto the low wall.

Rhys dropped down next to her. "Holy cow! You were amazing! Did you see him shaking?"

She laughed weakly. "Teeth. You knocked out one of his teeth."

"Ha!" He scrubbed his face. "Yeah, that felt good, not gonna lie."

Niamh buried her face in Rhys' shoulder, and he held her. They sat, quietly, just breathing, for several minutes until he spoke.

"Niamh, I'm so sorry. About all of this. If you don't want to go this morning I understand."

She remembered his conversation with Ian the first day he'd asked her out. How upset he'd been that his then-girlfriend broke up with him not because of her own feelings, but because of outside voices. She lifted her head. They may have only met this week, but she wasn't about to let someone like Alan Tildale influence how she felt, or what she did or didn't do with Rhys. And Rhys needed to know it.

"Rhys, I'm not—"

"No, no," he interrupted, face earnest. "Don't listen to him. You *are*."

Niamh blinked, confused. "What?"

"Intelligent. And intuitive. And fascinating." He cupped her face in his hands. "And beautiful. You don't need to be in step with Tildale's world or anybody else's world. You're your own world. Don't let him convince you otherwise."

She drank in his face, stunned. The heat from his hands spread down her neck, across her shoulders. His heat, his light—over the last week she'd watched him freely share these things. Niamh took his hands in hers and lowered them from her face but didn't release them. "Thank you. Although that's not what I was going to say."

It was his turn to look confused. "You weren't about to say you think you don't belong with me or something?"

She shook her head. "When we met, I thought anyone would feel dim next to you. You were this vibrant, electric ..." She paused, searching for the words. "Brightness. Like a comet. Or a sun with its own gravity that was sucking me towards it. And you were shooting sparks everywhere, and yes." She chuckled. "You are ridiculously attractive."

He ducked his head, some of his light returning.

"But the last several days," she went on. "Watching you with other people, like that boy on the beach, or Robbie, and spending time with you—Rhys, your light doesn't drown others out. It helps them to shine on their own. When I'm with you, I feel brighter."

"Wow," he breathed, glowing. "That's—thank you." He swallowed. "What were you going to say then?"

"I was going to say that Alan Tildale is a git. And I know he's hurt you before, and you've been worried about him ruining things again. But his nonsense isn't going to influence my feelings—either way. He can't bully me into not seeing you anymore—especially after this morning—but we're also not going to keep dating simply to prove him wrong. And he won't influence whether or not I sell The Nook and Cranny. He doesn't get to write the next part of my story."

Rhys exhaled slowly, worry lines on his forehead smoothing. "I can't tell you what a relief that is." He didn't comment on the idea of not dating anymore, although she'd seen his quick half frown when she'd said it. She meant both halves of that idea. Alan didn't get any sway over them, but she did still have a choice to make by the end of today. And long-distance relationships didn't work. Rhys had said she was her own world—she didn't even try to deny the thrill that gave her—but she didn't yet know if her world could merge with his.

For now, she gripped his hand and marched them to a garbage can on the sidewalk. She pinched Alan's paper between two fingers, dangled it over the trash can, and let it drop.

"Now," she said. "What fabulous adventures do you have planned for us this morning?"

He smiled and the warmth of it bathed her face like the sunrise. "It's a surprise."

They pulled into a wide field outside of town just as the eastern sky began to lighten. Niamh made out two figures in the middle of the field wrestling with what looked like a giant piece of fabric.

She squinted through the darkness. Yellow flames shot up, rippling the fabric. "Is that a hot air balloon?"

Rhys' eyes sparkled. "It is. I thought a little perspective might help you figure out what to do with that deadline of yours." He grabbed a backpack from the back seat and came around to open her door. As they jogged toward it, the balloon filled and floated upright. Two operators in company polo shirts helped them into the basket with the pilot. Heat radiated from the fire blowing into the balloon, and Rhys' fingers warmed hers.

Niamh thought she could get used to being warm.

The ground crew unlatched the tethers, the balloon lifted, and the world fell away. Life on the ground shrank and flattened. The city came into view in the distance, a faraway world of lights and people going about their lives. The Nook and Cranny was down there, in that world. But was it still her world? It hurt, this not knowing if she still belonged in her Tir na nÓg.

Next to her, Rhys took a thermos and mugs from his pack and cleared his throat. "I made you something. Or rather, I added something to what you made. Your tea blend, the one for decisions."

Her eyebrows lifted. "You did? For me?"

He nodded. Behind him tendrils of pink light began to creep over the hills. "There's this plant back east, where I'm from, called staghorn. You can make this kind of lemonade-tasting drink out of the berries. My mom's a textile artist. She uses it as a natural fixative, to make the colors stick. I thought it might, you know, help decisions to stick."

"Rhys, thank you. That's brilliant." Niamh took the mug, cinnamon and the staghorn's lemon rising in the steam. She pictured the contract on her desk, focused on the different paths that accepting or rejecting could bring, and sipped the tea. The sun crested the hills in the east, and dawn colored the sky. Lavender and rose spread to the west, where the moon, just full, was still in the sky. Its silver blended with the sunrise colors around it.

Niamh caught her breath. "The moon is still up."

Rhys followed her gaze. "Oh, yeah. I love it when the moon is full in the morning. It's beautiful. Although I have been known to draw a mustache or two on the moon too." He wiggled his eyebrows.

She laughed, flipping her gaze between east and west. "They're both here. Sun and moon at the same time." She knew perfectly well that the full moon didn't set until after sunrise, but it had never hit her like this. Even knowing, if someone had asked her before that moment whether the moon belonged in the night or the day, she would have answered night without hesitation. The moon in the daytime would be out of step, out of place. Right?

Yet here it was, in the same sky—the same world—as the rising sun, perfectly at home. Right where it belonged. She laughed again and drank more of the tea. "Of course they're both here."

"Niamh," Rhys said. "I wanted to tell you something."

She tore her eyes away from the celestial epiphany happening in front of her to look him in the eyes. "Yes?"

"I keep thinking about the Niamh in the legend, and about what you said. What *did* she do? Did she still feel like she belonged in Tír na nÓg? Or did she leave it for Oisin's world? And would that new world have been able to really see her? And I think, and this is just me, but I think that she belongs in whatever world she wants to be in. And that world is lucky to have her. *You* belong in whatever world you want to be in." He set her now empty mug on the basket floor. "You were honest with me about Alan not influencing us either way, and about the fact that that included the possibility of us not seeing each other anymore, so I'm going to be honest too. I meant what I said this morning. You are intelligent, wise, you're beautiful, and you fascinate me. Whatever you decide to do about the café—sell or not sell—I hope you decide to see if we can be in the same world."

Niamh was silent, eyes wide and heart jumping. The balloon cleared a rise, and a gust of wind rocked the basket. She stumbled, and Rhys reached out a hand to catch her. The sun moved behind him, haloing his head. Sunrise heat, all bright blue and vibrant orange, blazed around him. He stood, hand outstretched, light shining, like the Niamh of legend must have appeared to Oisin. An invitation to a new world.

New doesn't have to be a place. The thought came with clarity and a faint scent of lemon. *New doesn't have to be a place, and a person can be an entire world.*

"I think we can," she whispered.

Later, she would tell him about this exact moment, the moment she fell in love with him. For now, she had plenty of time. This was, after all, only their third date. And The

Nook and Cranny wasn't going anywhere. Niamh pulled Rhys close and kissed him, leaving her old world behind and running into a new one.

About the author

Kelly Fae Wilson writes unique, feel-good, romantic sci-fi and fantasy. Outside of writing, you can find her teaching dance, playing with faeries, or instigating a food fight at the dinner table. She lives with her husband and kids in Northern Utah. Find her at https://www.kellyfaewilson.com/